POSTCARDS FROM IMPOSSIBLE WORLDS

The Collected Shortest Story

// PETER CHIYKOWSKI //

Distributed in Canada by:

Fitzhenry & Whiteside Limited
195 Allstate Parkway
Markham, Ontario L3R 4T8
Phone: (905) 477-9700
e-mail: bookinfo@fitzhenry.ca

Printed in Canada.
CIP data available upon request.

Distributed in the U.S. by:

Consortium Book Sales & Distribution
34 Thirteenth Avenue, NE, Suite 101
Minneapolis, MN 55413
Phone: (612) 746-2600
e-mail: sales.orders@cbsd.com

THE SHORTEST STORY
Toronto, Canada
http://shorteststory.com
peter@shorteststory.com

CHIZINE PUBLICATIONS
Peterborough Canada
http://chizinepub.com
info@chizinepub.com

First Edition
ISBN 978-1-77148-467-1 (tpb)

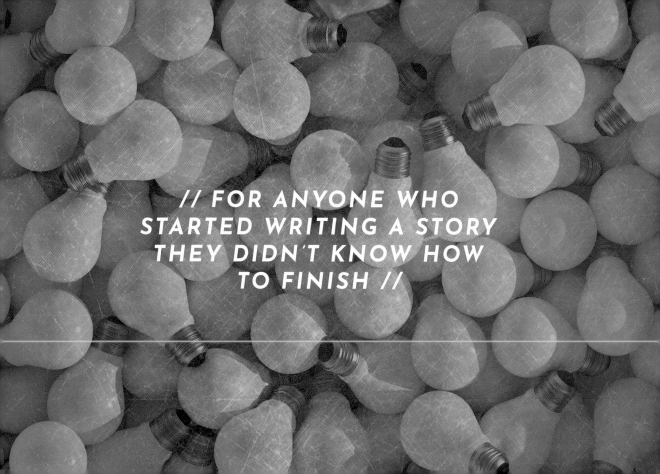

// FOR ANYONE WHO STARTED WRITING A STORY THEY DIDN'T KNOW HOW TO FINISH //

// FOREWORD //

Peter Chiykowski is that rare soul who makes you wonder why we ever gave up the general word *artist* for the more specific *writer*. Chiykowski's multi-genre work in short fiction, poetry, music, webcomics both serial and discrete, and whatever hybrid forms his magician's fingers will find tomorrow knows, yes, that each genre has its unique essence but also its transferrable play and wonder. His insatiable creativity keeps finding new arenas in which to do the artist's tireless work with keen-eyed social observation, with truths private and public. Let him, as he does here, braid observation and extrapolation, the endured and the imagined. "I'm an artist," John Lennon insists in one *Rolling Stone* interview (not "I'm a *musician*"): "I'm an artist, and if you give me a tuba, I'll bring you something out of it." Wash Chiykowski up on that clichéd deserted island and he'll bring you something out of fruit husks and charcoal. Chiykowski can always find treasure; lucky us, he shares it.

All that, and he's hilarious. Or rather, he's hilarious *because* of all that. Clive James knows, "Common sense and a sense of humour are the same thing, moving at different speeds. A sense of humour is just common sense, dancing." Oh, the beautiful dance, the reach and flashing speed, of *Postcards from Impossible Worlds*.

Darryl Whetter, Programme Leader, MA Creative Writing, LASALLE College of the Arts, Singapore

// THE TELEPHONE //

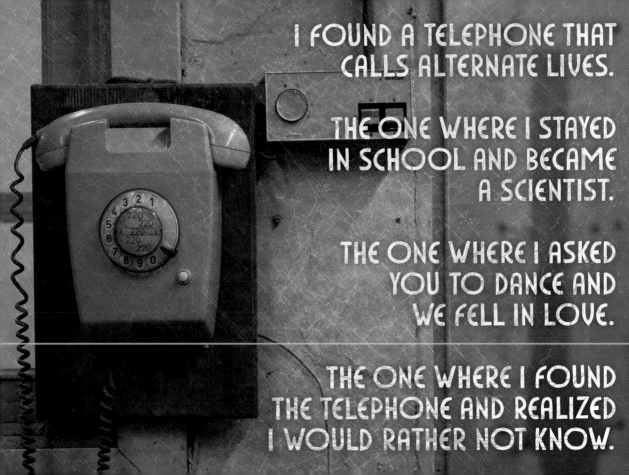

// THE RIDDLE OF THE SPHINX //

WHAT WALKS ON FOUR LEGS IN THE MORNING,
TWO LEGS AT NOON, AND THREE LEGS IN THE
EVENING?

BECAUSE IT'S EVOLVING
QUICKLY, THE LEGS ARE
GROWING BACK, AND
THIS BUNKER DOOR
WON'T HOLD
FOREVER.

// SWORDS INTO
PLOWSHARES //

// THE DAY THE OCEANS DISAPPEARED //

ONE MORNING WE WOKE TO FIND THE OCEANS HAD DISAPPEARED.

WE WALKED PAST GASPING FISH AND GAZED INTO TRENCHES SO VAST THAT THEIR SILENCE SEEMED AS OLD AS THE EARTH ITSELF.

AND ALL THE WHILE, THE MEN WHO OWN THE WORLD ARGUED OVER WHO GOT TO BUILD THE FIRST DEEP-SEA CONDO COMPLEX.

// IS THIS DOLL HAUNTED? //

"EXCUSE ME,
IS THIS DOLL
HAUNTED?"
I ASKED.

"NO," SAID
THE SHOPKEEPER.

"OF COURSE NOT,"
SAID THE DOLL.

// BLOOD IN THE WATER //

// OCTOPUS FACTS //

HELLO. I AM SCIENTIST IN OCTOPUS SCIENCE
LABORATORY HERE ARE SOME OCTOPUS FACTS

ONE: OCTOPUS CAN SQUEEZE THROUGH ONE-INCH HOLE

TWO: OCTOPUS CAN CHANGE COLOUR AND SHAPE FOR
DISGUISE LIKE PREDATOR OR ROCK OR SCIENTIST IN
OCTOPUS SCIENCE LABORATORY

THREE: SCIENCE OCTOPUS IS MISSING NO ONE KNOWS
WHERE IS HAHA

NOW IS YOUR TURN FOR TELL ME SOME HUMAN FACTS:
HOW MANY ARMS DOES HUMAN LEADER HAVE?

// BURNING, BURNING //

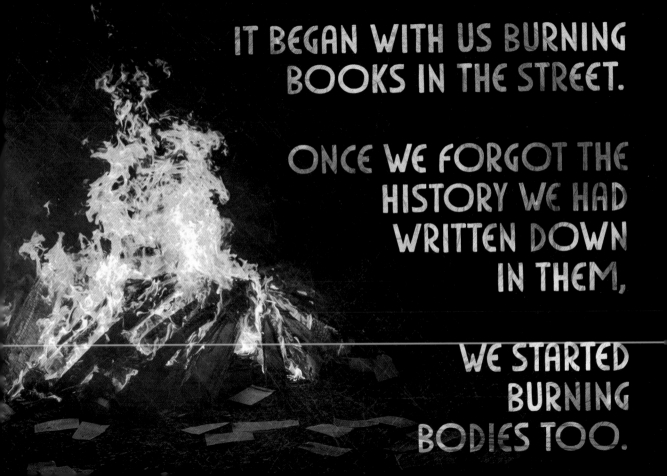

// THE TOWN
WITH NO NAME //

ALL THREE OF US WERE SILENT AS WE DROVE PAST THE BLANK "WELCOME TO" SIGN AND INTO THE TOWN WITH NO NAME.

THE PEOPLE ALL WATCHED US WITH THE SAME SLACK EXPRESSION, THEIR HEADS TILTED AT IDENTICAL ANGLES AS IF LISTENING TO A SINGLE FAR-OFF SOUND.

FOR A MOMENT, I HEARD IT TOO.

FOR A MOMENT, THE PEOPLE IN THE CAR SEEMED LIKE STRANGERS AND I COULDN'T REMEMBER WHO WE WERE OR WHERE WE WERE GOING, BUT THEN WE PASSED THE LAST HOUSE AND IT CAME BACK.

WE WERE ALL OLD FRIENDS. ALL TRAVELLING TOGETHER. ALL SAFE.

ALL FOUR OF US.

// MACHINE TIME THE //

ACCIDENT MACHINE

TIME TERRIBLE THAT

FROM YOU SAVE I

WHERE WORLD THE

TO BACK WAY

MY FIND CAN I

BEFORE MACHINE TIME

MY REBUILD AND BREAK

I MUST

TIMES MANY HOW?

// CAREER PLAN //

MY CAREER PLAN IS TO FIND A SUITCASE FULL OF DRUG MONEY AND SPEND THE REST OF MY LIFE DRUNK BY THE OCEAN.

WHY, THINK YOU'RE DOING BETTER AS A HIGH SCHOOL GUIDANCE COUNSELLOR?

// SOIL //

guest story by James Mark Miller

I FOUND THE SECRET LANGUAGE OF THE EARTH,
AND IT BENT TO MY COMMAND.

I SHIFTED STONES AND SOIL.
MOVED MOUNTAINS.

BUT WHEN I WENT TO
YOUR GRAVE TO ASK
THE SOIL TO RETURN YOU,
THE FLOWERS YOU LOVED
WERE GROWING
THERE.

AND I REALIZED
IT ALREADY HAD.

// THE SHUTTLE //

MAYBE IT'S JUST THE SPACE MADNESS TALKING, BUT EVERYTHING SEEMS SO PEACEFUL WHEN YOU'RE *FINALLY* ALONE UP HERE.

NO MORE WAR.

NO MORE FAMINE.

NO MORE MISSION PARTNER EATING ALL THE GOOD OATMEAL PACKETS AND LEAVING YOU WITH CINNAMON.

// MIRROR UNIVERSE //

I FOUND A PORTAL TO A
UNIVERSE WHERE EVERYTHING
IS BACKWARDS.

TELEVISIONS WATCH US.
BANKS ROB PEOPLE.
COPS KILL THE INNOCENT.

WAIT, WHY AM I
TELLING YOU?

YOU LIVE THERE.

// THE VOLUNTEER //

EVERYONE PUTS THEIR HAND UP WHEN YOU ASK WHO WANTS TO BE RICH AND POWERFUL.

EVERYONE PUTS THEIR HAND UP WHEN YOU ASK WHO WANTS TO LIVE FOREVER.

BUT OH BOY, ASK FOR A VOLUNTEER TO SACRIFICE A COUPLE VIRGINS AND SUDDENLY EVERYONE IS STARING AT THEIR PHONES.

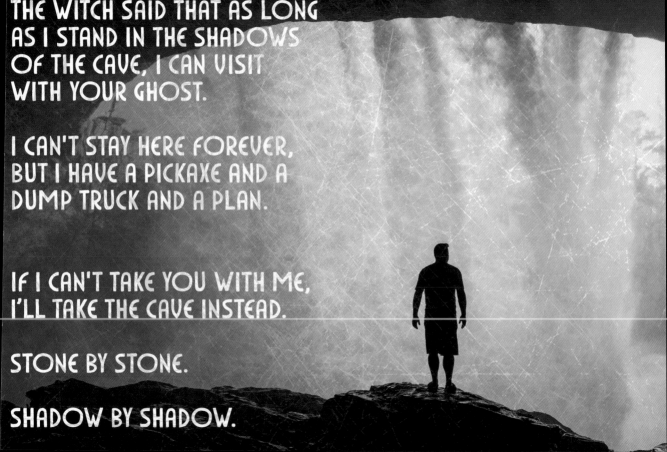

// THE BOY CAME BACK ALL WRONG //

hear this story narrated by Cecil Baldwin at
shorteststory.com/boy

THE BOY CAME BACK ALL WRONG, HIS STEP AN UNEVEN, LURCHING DANCE, LIKE A WAGON WITH SQUARE WHEELS.

IN PUBLIC, HIS PARENTS SAID THEY WERE JUST GRATEFUL TO HAVE THEIR SON BACK.

IN PRIVATE, THEY CLUTCHED THEIR STAKES AND WONDERED WHY THE FIRST ATTEMPT DIDN'T TAKE.

// THE ISLAND
OF LOST DOGS //

MY LIFEBOAT WASHED UP
ON THE ENCHANTED ISLAND
WHERE ALL LOST DOGS GO.

I FOUND MY NEIGHBOUR'S
HUSKY AND MY GRANDMA'S
OLD PUG AND I CAN HEAR MY
CHILDHOOD BASSET HOUND
BARKING SOMEWHERE
IN THE DISTANCE.

I PROMISE TO BRING NEWS
OF THEIR WHEREABOUTS WHEN
I RETURN HOME, BUT FIRST
THERE ARE TUMMIES TO RUB
AND NAPS TO SHARE AND
WHO AM I KIDDING?

I'M ALREADY HOME.

// 100·MILE DIET //

WHEN WE STARTED TRADING WITH OTHER PLANETS, THE 100-MILE DIET ALL BUT DISAPPEARED.

IT WASN'T BECAUSE ALIEN FOOD IS CHEAPER,

BUT BECAUSE WE TURNED EVERY LAST SCRAP OF PLANET INTO SHOPPING MALLS THE MOMENT WE DIDN'T NEED SOIL TO SURVIVE.

// STOLEN HEART //

hear this story narrated by Cecil Baldwin at
shorteststory.com/heart

I STILL REMEMBER THE EXACT MOMENT I REALIZED YOU HAD STOLEN MY HEART.

YOU WERE STANDING THERE, THE BONES OF MY VANQUISHED TOMB-GUARD STREWN ABOUT YOU, MY ORGAN RELIQUARY SHATTERED AT YOUR FEET.

SOMETIMES YOU

// WITCH HUNT //

PEOPLE ARE FAR TOO
QUICK TO JOIN
A WITCH HUNT.

YOU TURN ONE
NEIGHBOURHOOD KID
INTO A SHRIEKING PUMPKIN
AND IT'S LIKE THAT'S ALL THEY
CAN TALK ABOUT.

// THE ALIENS' PERSPECTIVE //

MAYBE FROM
THE ALIENS' PERSPECTIVE, WE
ARE THE DANGEROUS INVADERS.

BUT THEN AGAIN, MAYBE WE'RE
THE DEFENCELESS PLANET OF LIVING
BLOOD BAGS THEY USE TO
SPAWN THEIR YOUNG.

ACTUALLY, I'M PRETTY SURE
IT'S THE SECOND ONE.

// THE NIGHT OF THE RED SAILS //

THERE'S A TRADITION AROUND HERE WE DON'T TELL THE CITY PEOPLE ABOUT.

ON THE FIRST NEW MOON OF THE YEAR, OUR VILLAGE TAKES TO THE WATER WITH CRIMSON LANTERNS THAT MARK OUR BOATS SAFE FROM THE LADY OF THE SHALLOWS.

WE ALWAYS BRING ONE OUTSIDER WITH US. WE MUST EXPLAIN TO HIM WHAT WE ARE DOING BEFORE WE LOWER HIM INTO THE WATER. THAT'S IMPORTANT. IT'S NOT THE FLESH SHE FEEDS ON, YOU SEE. IT'S THE FEAR.

IF SHE DOESN'T GET HER FILL, SHE COULD COME BACK EARLY. SHE COULD TAKE ONE OF *US*. SO PLEASE UNDERSTAND, THERE'S NOTHING PERSONAL ABOUT THIS. CAREFUL NOW, MIND THE ROPES AS YOU GO DOWN.

YES, THAT'S IT. THAT'S THE FEAR. OUR LADY WILL FEED WELL TONIGHT.

OH, DON'T CURSE NOW. YOU CAME TO OUR SWEET LITTLE VILLAGE TO TELL US HOW QUAINT WE ARE, TO GET YOUR FILL OF OUR SMALL-TOWN WAYS AND GO HOME WITH A STORY.

WELL THESE ARE OUR WAYS. THIS IS YOUR STORY.

IT'S NOT OUR FAULT IF YOU DON'T LIKE HOW IT ENDS.

// ETHICS COMMITTEE //

hear this story narrated by Cecil Baldwin at
shorteststory.com/ethics

IS IT WRONG TO TAMPER WITH HUMAN D.N.A.?

IS IT WRONG TO MURDER AN ENTIRE ETHICS COMMITTEE?

IS IT WRONG TO REPLACE THEM WITH OBEDIENT LABORATORY CLONES?

I LEAVE THESE QUESTIONS IN THE CAPABLE HANDS OF THE ETHICS COMMITTEE.

// LIBERTY TRIUMPHANT //

IT'S BEEN THREE DAYS SINCE THE
STATUE OF LIBERTY CAME TO LIFE,

HER GREAT COPPER LEGS THUNDERING
DOWN INTERSTATE 95,

HER MONSTROUS STEPS
SHAKING THE COASTLINE,

HER ANGRY JAWS CHEWING UP EVERY
CORRUPT C.E.O. AND POLITICIAN
ON THE ROAD TO WASHINGTON.

I FEEL LIKE A PATRIOT AGAIN.

// WE GREW UP WITH PROPHECIES //

guest story by Jordan Shiveley

YOU HAD BEEN RAISED WITH THE WORDS OF THE PROPHECIES RINGING IN YOUR EARS. YOU KNEW THAT ONE DAY, A GREAT DARKNESS WOULD ARISE, AND THAT YOU WOULD HAVE TO FACE IT. SO YOU TRAINED. YOU STUDIED THE GRIMOIRES, BOUND YOUR HAIR BACK AND SMEARED THE SYMBOLS THAT REQUIRED BLOOD AND ASH. AND THOSE PROPHECIES...

WELL, THEY CAME TRUE...

EXCEPT THEY GOT ONE THING WRONG. THE DARKNESS HAD BEEN RIGHT THERE, STARING YOU IN THE FACE ALL ALONG...

SMILING.

// THE PRINCESS AND THE FROG //

EVERY MORNING I GO DOWN
TO THE LAKE TO SEE
THE FROG PRINCE.

I TELL PEOPLE THAT
ONE DAY HE'LL TURN
INTO A HUMAN.

IT'S EASIER THAN
EXPLAINING

SOME PRINCESSES
ARE INTO FROGS.

// THE WISHING DICE //

THE FIRST TIME I USED THE WISHING DICE, I ASKED FOR A CHILD.
I ROLLED EVENS. A YEAR LATER, MY DAUGHTER WAS BORN.

THE SECOND TIME, I ASKED FOR A BIGGER HOME. I ROLLED ODDS.
MY HOUSE BURNED DOWN WITH MY FAMILY INSIDE.

THE LAST TIME, I HELD THE DICE OVER THE STAIRWELL
OF MY NEW APARTMENT, HALF WISHING
FOR THE COURAGE TO THROW THEM
AWAY, HALF WISHING TO SEE MY
FAMILY AGAIN.

I SHUT MY EYES AND DROPPED THEM.

I DON'T KNOW WHICH WISH THE DICE HEARD,
BUT I KNOW THAT YEARS LATER, I STILL
LIE AWAKE AT NIGHT, WAITING TO HEAR
IF THEY'LL EVER HIT THE GROUND.

// AFTER THE BOMBS //

AFTER THE BOMBS FELL, WE MADE FOR THE
COAST, SURPRISED TO FIND THE SKY ALIVE
WITH THE CALLS OF SEA BIRDS AND THE
OCEAN CHURNING WITH NEW LIFE THAT
LOOKED STRANGE AND DARK AND BEAUTIFUL,

LIKE BREAKING AN EGG AND LOOKING DOWN
TO DISCOVER WE HAD MADE AN OMELETTE.

// FOLLOW THE TRACKS //

hear this story narrated by Cecil Baldwin at shorteststory.com/tracks

WHEN THE WORLD FELL, THE LAST THING MY MOTHER TOLD ME WAS "FOLLOW THE TRACKS..."

I WALKED THROUGH DEAD CITIES AND EMPTY TOWNS...

"FOLLOW THE TRACKS..."

PAST TREES OF HANGED MEN AND CAMPSITES STREWN WITH CORPSES...

"FOLLOW THE TRACKS..."

I KILLED AND BLED AND STITCHED MYSELF UP MORE TIMES THAN I COULD COUNT BEFORE I REALIZED THAT MY MOTHER NEVER KNEW WHERE THE TRACKS LED.

BUT SHE KNEW THAT HELL IS EASIER TO WALK THROUGH WHEN YOU PICK A DIRECTION.

// I WON'T BE AFRAID //

I HEAR THEM CALLING IN THE PIPES AFTER
SUNDOWN, THEIR VOICES TOO STICKY AND
TOO SWEET, LIKE PLUMS GONE TO ROT.

ONE NIGHT I AWAKE TO FIND MYSELF
SLEEPWALKING TOWARD THE SEWER. THE NEXT
TIME, MY FINGERS ARE WRAPPED AROUND
THE COLD METAL GRATE, POISED TO LIFT.

I KNOW IT'S JUST A MATTER OF TIME
UNTIL MY VOICE JOINS THEM
DOWN THERE IN THE DARKNESS.

IT'S OKAY, THOUGH.

I CAN ALREADY TELL THAT BY
THEN, I WON'T BE AFRAID.

// SUPER-HEARING //

I WOULD LOVE TO SIT HERE WHILE YOU TELL ME HOW MY MUTANT POWERS GIVE ME A DUTY TO HELP SAVE THIS CITY FROM CERTAIN DOOM,

BUT MY GIFT IS SUPER-HEARING.

YOU'RE LOOKING FOR SOMEONE WITH SUPER-LISTENING.

OR SUPER-CARING.

// WOKE UP IN THE WRECKAGE //

I WOKE UP IN THE WRECKAGE WITH YOUR NAME ON MY LIPS AND BODIES ALL AROUND ME.

I REMEMBERED THE SHUDDER OF THE PLANE PITCHING DOWNWARD, FREEFALL PULLING AIR FROM MY LUNGS.

I REMEMBERED THE DELIRIOUS MOMENT I TURNED TO THE SEAT NEXT TO ME AND SAW THE SMILING MAN.

"SAY A NAME," HE SAID TO ME. "GIVE ME A NAME AND I'LL MAKE SURE YOU LIVE."

I WOKE UP IN THE WRECKAGE WITH YOUR NAME ON MY LIPS AND BODIES ALL AROUND ME, AND I KNEW WITHOUT LOOKING THAT THE ONE IN THE SEAT NEXT TO ME WAS

// DON'T RESCUE ME //

I ALWAYS WAIT FOR
THE SEARCH PLANES TO
LEAVE BEFORE I LIGHT
THE SIGNAL FLARE.

I LIKE BEING ALONE
ON THIS ISLAND. I DON'T
WANT THEM TO RESCUE ME.

BUT IN CASE THEY DO, IT SHOULD
AT LEAST LOOK LIKE I TRIED.

// RESORTED TO CANNIBALISM //

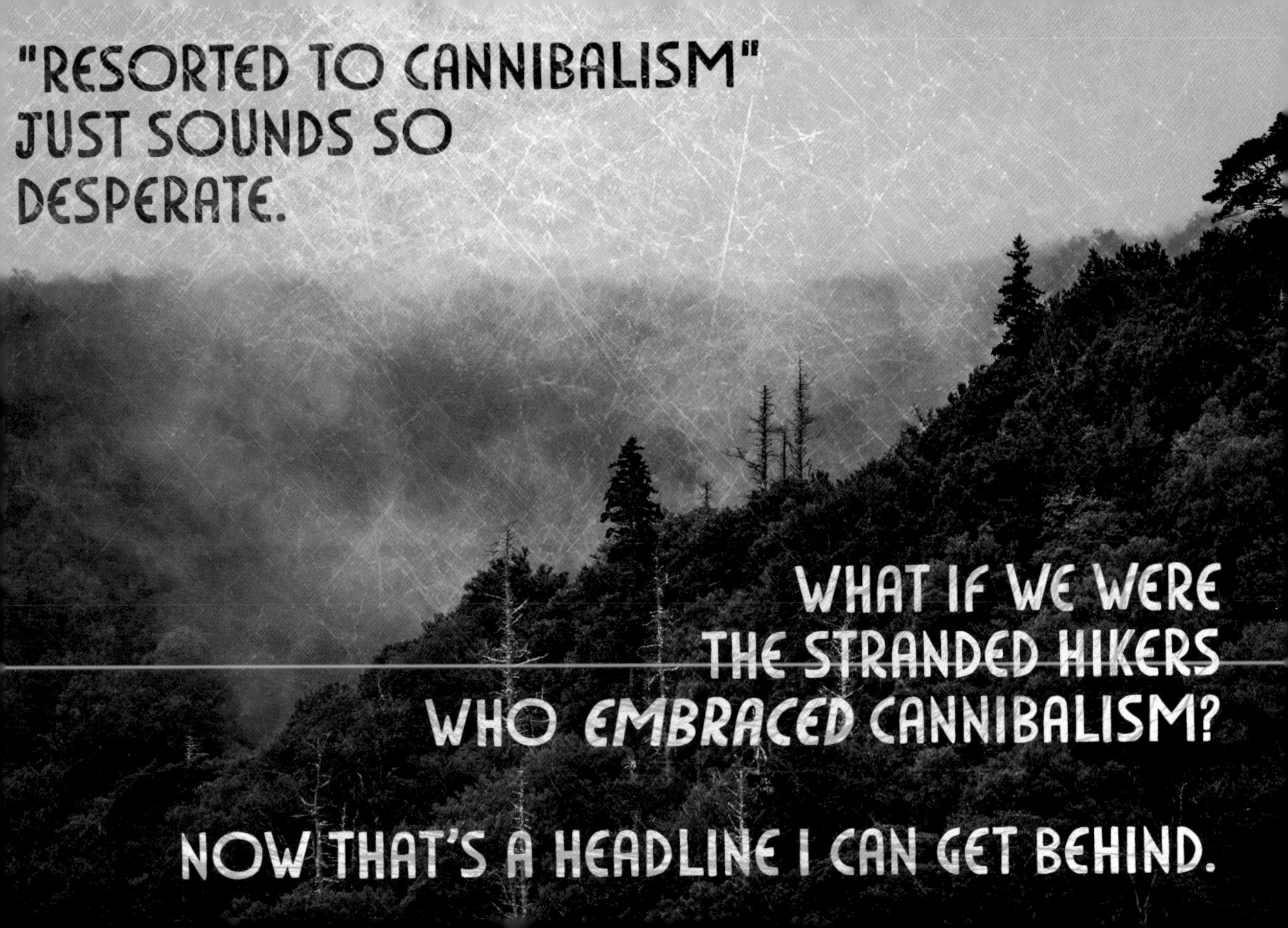
"RESORTED TO CANNIBALISM"
JUST SOUNDS SO
DESPERATE.
WHAT IF WE WERE
THE STRANDED HIKERS
WHO EMBRACED CANNIBALISM?
NOW THAT'S A HEADLINE I CAN GET BEHIND.

// THE FOREST WHISPERED //

hear this story narrated by Cecil Baldwin at
shorteststory.com/forest

"WE SHOULD TURN BACK," YOU SAID.

YOUR WORDS MADE SENSE,
BUT THE FOREST WHISPERED,
"FURTHER, FURTHER."

AND OUR FEET
COULD NOT HELP
BUT LISTEN.

// ALIEN JUNK DRAWER //

ALIEN ARTEFACTS HAVE STARTED APPEARING INSIDE MY JUNK DRAWER:

MATCHBOX-SIZED SPACESHIPS, BOTTLE OPENERS FOR NON-ORIENTABLE TWO-DIMENSIONAL MANIFOLDS, SUNGLASSES FOR WATCHING THE ELECTROMAGNETIC SPECTRUM SHATTER DURING THE DEATH OF A STAR.

I AM GOING TO USE THEM TO EXPLORE THE WONDERS OF OUR VAST AND MYSTERIOUS UNIVERSE.

NEXT YEAR. IF I HAVE TIME.

// RUSTLING GREEN //

AT FIRST IT WAS JUST A FOOT THAT GREW IN MY GARDEN,
SO SOFT AND SUPPLE IN THE RUSTLING GREEN.

SOON THE REST TOOK SHAPE: A LEG, LONG AND DELICATE,

HIPS BLOOMING OUTWARD LIKE AN INK BLOT TEST,

A SPINE, KNOTTED AND BOWED LIKE A STRING OF BLUEBELLS,

FINALLY
I COULD SEE
MY STRANGE FRUIT,

HER HAIR AS BROWN, HER DRESS AS BRIGHT, HER EYES AS
DARK AND WILD AS THE DAY SHE WAS PLANTED.

// MAGIC RING //

I FOUND A MAGIC RING THAT LETS ME PINPOINT
THE EXACT WORD SOMEONE IS
STRUGGLING TO THINK OF.

AT FIRST I USED IT WHENEVER I COULD,
AND MY FRIENDS THANKED ME.

BUT SOON I BEGAN TO SEE
THEIR JAWS TWITCH, HOW
THEY BRISTLED LIKE
GUNDOGS, HUNGRIER
FOR THE CHASE THAN
FOR THE KILL.

AND SO I PUT THE RING
AWAY, AND AGAIN, MY
FRIENDS THANKED ME.

// APTITUDE TEST //

AT FIRST WE THOUGHT THE APTITUDE TESTS WERE TO SPOT THE INFECTED.

WE'D SEEN HOW FAST THE VIRUS COULD DISABLE THE BRAIN. MAYBE THEY WERE CATCHING IT EARLY. MAYBE THOSE SMALL GREEN VIALS OF ANTIVIRUS COULD KEEP US SAFE.

BUT THEN I SAW HOW MANY OF US HAD GATHERED AT THE TREATMENT CENTRE,

AND HOW FEW OF THOSE SMALL GREEN VIALS REMAINED.

AND I KNEW.

THEY WERE JUST SEEING WHO WAS WORTH SAVING.

// THE BEACH OF LOST THINGS //

AFTER THE SHIPWRECK, I WOKE UP ON THE DISTANT BEACH WHERE ALL THE THINGS WE LOSE WILL ONE DAY WASH UP.

I LOOKED OUT OVER MILES OF GLITTERING CAR KEYS, SUNGLASSES, CELLPHONES AND LOOSE COINS, AND FELT A STRANGE PEACE THINKING,

EVERYTHING CAN BE REPLACED.

EVEN ME.

// UNFINISHED BUSINESS //

guest story by Helen Marshall

A BOY I DATED ONCE HAD A SWAN WING IN
PLACE OF HIS ARM.

HE GOT IT FROM A GIRL WAY BACK, BAD
BREAK UP— THAT OLD STORY, YOU KNOW?

IT NEVER CAME TO MUCH BETWEEN US BUT
SOMETIMES I REMEMBER THE FEEL OF HIM.

NOT EVERYONE WEARS THEIR
UNFINISHED BUSINESS
SO OPENLY.

// CONTAINMENT PROTOCOL //

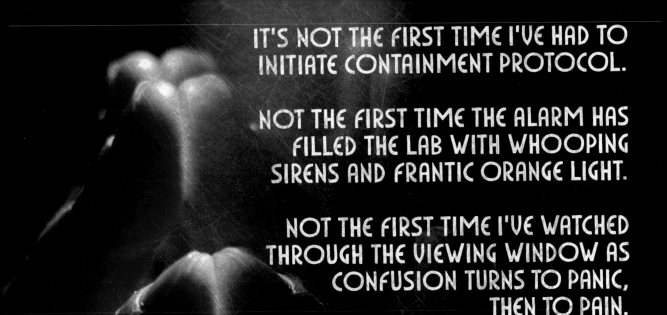

IT'S NOT THE FIRST TIME I'VE HAD TO INITIATE CONTAINMENT PROTOCOL.

NOT THE FIRST TIME THE ALARM HAS FILLED THE LAB WITH WHOOPING SIRENS AND FRANTIC ORANGE LIGHT.

NOT THE FIRST TIME I'VE WATCHED THROUGH THE VIEWING WINDOW AS CONFUSION TURNS TO PANIC, THEN TO PAIN.

IT ALL JUST SEEMS SO DIFFERENT NOW,

ON THIS SIDE OF THE GLASS.

// READ FAST, DIE OLD //

READ FAST,

DIE OLD,

LEAVE A MADDENING
LABYRINTH OF BOOKS.

// HIDE AND SEEK //

DAY 6: MADE CAMP IN SATELLITE CONTROL TOWER. FOUND GUN IN DESK. I SHOULD WELD DOOR SHUT AFTER I FIX GENERATOR. DON'T TRUST MYSELF NOT TO OPEN FOR DANIEL.

DAY 9: GENERATOR WORKING. POWER LOW. FROM TOWER I SPOT SEEKERS IN SURROUNDING WHEAT FIELDS, WALKING WHO KNOWS WHERE. SATELLITE SHOWS DOZENS MORE. THOUGHT I SPOTTED DANIEL'S RED BASEBALL CAP IN TOWN 30 MILES OUT, BUT IMAGE GRAINY. NO SIGN OF HIDERS. NO SIGN OF ANYONE UNTOUCHED BY SICKNESS.

DAY 12: SAW HIDER RUNNING IN FIELD TODAY, SEEKER FOLLOWING CLOSE. GOT CAUGHT ON PERIMETER FENCE. HE BEGGED, "PLEASE, DIANA. YOU'RE SICK." SHE SMILED LIKE A CHILD AT PLAY. "READY OR NOT," SHE SAID. "HERE I COME." REMINDER: WELD DOOR SHUT.

DAY 15: GENERATOR AT 30%. PRETTY SURE I SPOTTED DANIEL ON SATELLITE 20 MILES OUT. WAS UP ALL NIGHT CRYING. HOW DOES THE SICKNESS PAIR HIDERS AND SEEKERS? HOW DOES IT KNOW WHO IT HURTS MOST TO RUN FROM?

DAY 17: DEFINITELY HIM. 12 MILES AND CLOSING. GENERATOR AT 12%. SHOULD CONSERVE POWER, BUT CAN'T. I KNOW HE'LL KILL ME, BUT IT COMFORTS ME TO WATCH HIM.

DAY 19: GENERATOR DEAD, BUT NO MATTER. DANIEL 6 MILES AWAY. STILL HAVEN'T WELDED DOOR SHUT. WHY NOT? MAYBE SICKNESS IS A GAME WITH RULES WE MUST FOLLOW. CAN HIDERS KILL THEIR SEEKER? I PRACTISE LOADING GUN.

DAY 20: WATCHING DANIEL APPROACH THROUGH BINOCULARS. LOOKS TOO THIN, TOO PALE, SMILING ALL WRONG, BUT I CAN'T LOOK AWAY. GUN IS LOADED, OILED. I CAN HEAR HIM ON THE STAIRS, NOW AT THE DOOR. "READY OR NOT," HE SAYS. I RAISE THE GUN, BUT I'M NOT SURE WHO I'M POINTING IT AT. OH MY BOY, MY SWEET DANIEL. HERE I COME.

// IF TEN YEARS AGO
YOU TOLD ME //

IF TEN YEARS AGO YOU TOLD ME WHAT MY LIFE WOULD LOOK LIKE TODAY,

I WOULDN'T HAVE GUESSED "TRAPPED IN A SEA GOD'S PRISON FOR MAKING OUT WITH ALL THREE OF HIS WISH-GRANTING MERMAID DAUGHTERS."

BUT I WOULDN'T HAVE BEEN SURPRISED EITHER.

// THE MANNEQUINS' BALL //

THE MANNEQUINS'
BALL HAPPENS
ONCE A YEAR.

WE COME TO LIFE
FOR A SINGLE NIGHT
AND TRY TO IMITATE
EVERYTHING WE'VE
OBSERVED ABOUT HUMAN BEHAVIOUR.

WE GOSSIP. WE TRY ON CLOTHES. WE DRINK
IN THE CHANGE ROOM AND TALK SHIT
ABOUT THE SALES HELP.

AND WHEN NO ONE
IS AROUND, WE STAND
IN FRONT OF THE
MIRROR AND WISH
WE HAD EYES
TO CRY WITH.

MY REALITY
SIMULATOR
GOT MOST OF
YOU RIGHT.

YOUR VOICE,
YOUR SMILE,
THE WAY YOU SIGH
WHEN I TELL
A BAD JOKE.

BUT NOT THE
SMELL OF YOUR
HAIR WHEN YOU
WAKE UP NEXT TO ME
IN THE MORNING.

AND GRIEF IS A STICKLER FOR DETAIL.

// LIFE ON THE SURFACE //

YES, THE FLOOD CONSUMED OUR HOMES.

YES, LIFE IS DIFFERENT NOW, STRUGGLING TO SURVIVE ON RECLAIMED OCEAN LINERS AND FLOATING CITIES.

BUT I CAN'T HELP BUT SMILE WHEN I THINK ABOUT FISH SWIMMING AND CORAL GROWING

IN THE SUBMERGED RUINS OF EVERY CORPORATION THAT DENIED CLIMATE CHANGE.

// HAUNTED
CALL CENTRE //

hear this story narrated by Cecil Baldwin at
shorteststory.com/call

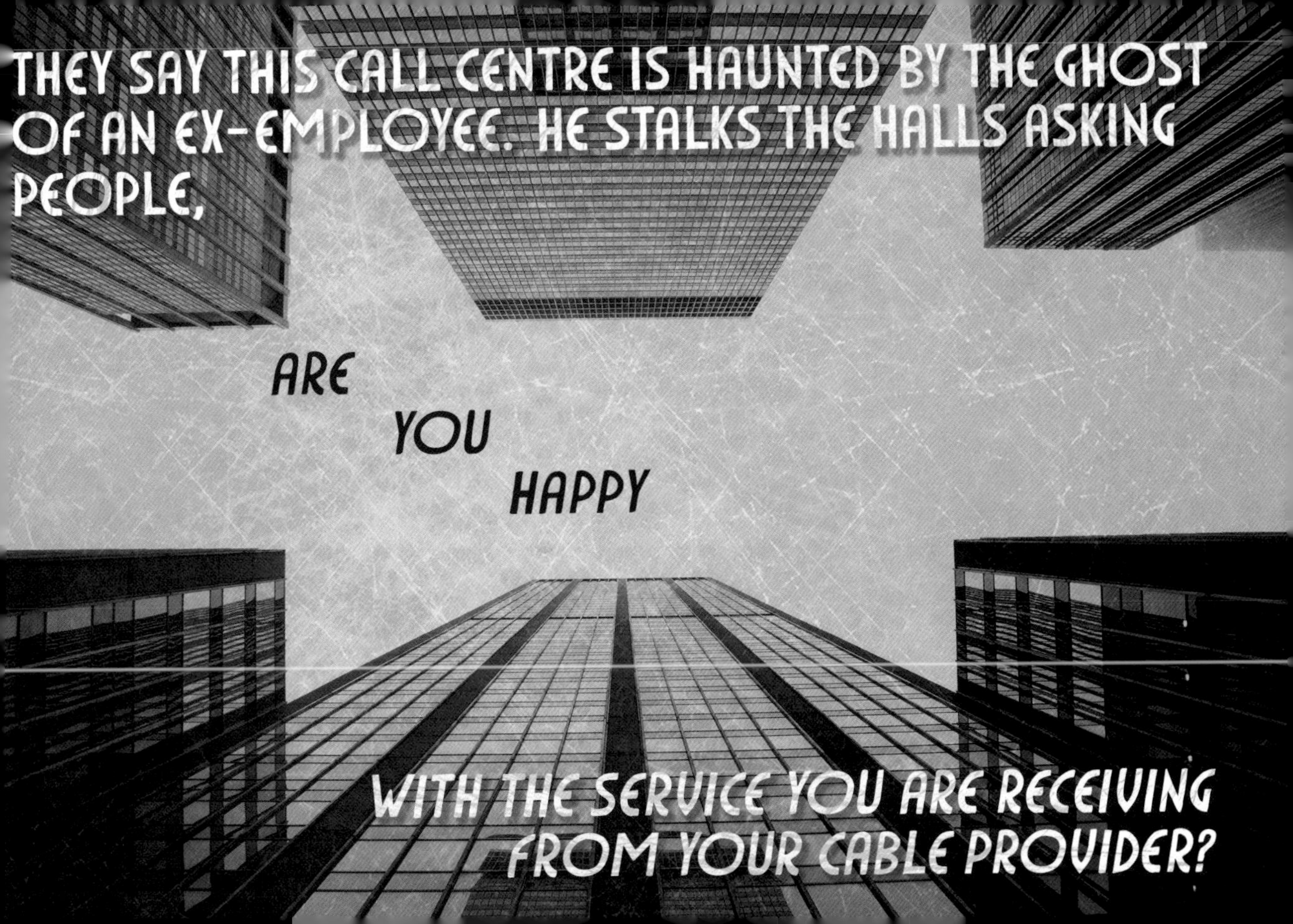
THEY SAY THIS CALL CENTRE IS HAUNTED BY THE GHOST OF AN EX-EMPLOYEE. HE STALKS THE HALLS ASKING PEOPLE,
ARE
YOU
HAPPY
WITH THE SERVICE YOU ARE RECEIVING FROM YOUR CABLE PROVIDER?

// SQUINT AND YOU'LL SEE ME //

guest story by Robert Shearman

ONLY TWO WEEKS INTO THE RELATIONSHIP, AND HE HAD ALREADY ECLIPSED HER. HE WAS SMARTER, KINDER, DRESSED MORE NATTILY, AND WAS BETTER AT TELLING JOKES. HE'D SOMETIMES LOOK OVER HIS SHOULDER, AND SEE HER SHIVERING IN THE DARKNESS OF HIS SHADOW, AND HE'D ASK, "ARE YOU ALL RIGHT?" AND SHE'D SHOUT BACK SHE WAS FINE, BUT HER VOICE DIDN'T TRAVEL VERY FAR, SHE WASN'T SURE HE COULD HEAR HER.

// THE INTERSECTION //

I DROVE OFF WITHOUT LOOKING BACK, VISION BLURRED AND HEAD SWIMMING.

I TRIED TO FOCUS ON FOLLOWING THE YELLOW LINES AWAY FROM TOWN, BUT SOMEWHERE TOOK A WRONG TURN BACK TO THE INTERSECTION. PEOPLE HAD GATHERED. A GURNEY HAD BEEN WHEELED OUT.

I REVERSED, TAKING BACKSTREETS TOWARD THE HIGHWAY, THINKING OF MY DAUGHTER WAITING AT HOME IN HER PINK SUNHAT. I ROUNDED THE CORNER AND FOUND MYSELF BACK AT THE INTERSECTION. THE CROWD HAD GROWN. I RECOGNIZED SOME OF THE FACES WATCHING ME IN THE LIGHT OF THE SIRENS.

BY THE THIRD TIME AROUND, I UNDERSTOOD. EACH TIME, I DROVE AWAY. EACH TIME, THE ROAD BROUGHT ME BACK. EACH TIME, THE INTERVAL WAS SHORTER, MY WORLD SMALLER.

FINALLY I PULLED INTO THE INTERSECTION AND ON EACH SIDE I SAW ANOTHER STREET LEADING TO ANOTHER INTERSECTION LEADING TO ANOTHER STREET WITH MY CAR IN THE MIDDLE, MY DRINK-FLUSHED FACE BEHIND THE WHEEL.

THIS IS MY WORLD NOW: AN INTERSECTION, A FLASHING SIREN, A PINK SUNHAT LYING IN THE ROAD.

// WILD THINGS //

WE ABANDONED OUR PROBLEMS AND WENT TO LIVE IN THE FOREST WITH THE WILD THINGS.

"WHY HAVE YOU COME HERE?" THE WILD THINGS ASKED.

"BECAUSE OUR HOME IS BESET BY THE TROUBLES OF FEARFUL, SHORTSIGHTED PEOPLE," WE REPLIED.

"AND YOUR TROUBLES WILL NOT FIND YOU HERE?"

"NOT FOR A LONG TIME," WE SAID.

"AND SO YOU'LL LIVE HERE, SHORTSIGHTED AND IN FEAR?"

AND WE STOOD FOR A MOMENT IN SILENCE.

"GO BACK TO YOUR HOME," THEY TOLD US. "FOR THAT IS WHERE WILD THINGS ARE NEEDED. FIGHT WITH TOOTH AND CLAW. LOVE WITH HEART AND WITH HACKLE. ROAR WITH ALL THE THUNDER IN YOUR LUNGS."

"AND THAT WILL BE THE END OF IT?" WE ASKED.

"NO," SAID THE WILD THINGS, "BUT IT WILL BE A START."

// **THE FOG** //

hear this story narrated by Cecil Baldwin at
shorteststory.com/fog

WHEN THE FOG CAME TO OUR TOWN, WE HEEDED THE WARNINGS AND GATHERED EVERY DAY TO COUNT OUR NUMBERS.

HOW PROUD WE WERE AFTER A WEEK WITH NO ONE TAKEN.

HOW PROUD AFTER A MONTH WITH ALL OF US ACCOUNTED FOR.

IT WAS ONLY WHEN THE FOG CLEARED THAT WE LOOKED OUT AT OUR PROUD TOWN AND SAW TOO MANY EMPTY HOMES.

IT WAS ONLY THEN THAT WE BEGAN TO REALIZE THE FOG HAD NOT SPARED US. WE HAD SIMPLY FORGOTTEN THE ONES IT TOOK.

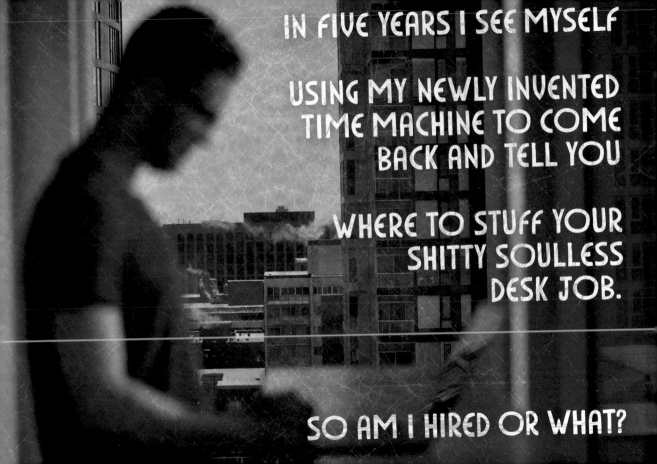

// TIRED OF WAITING //

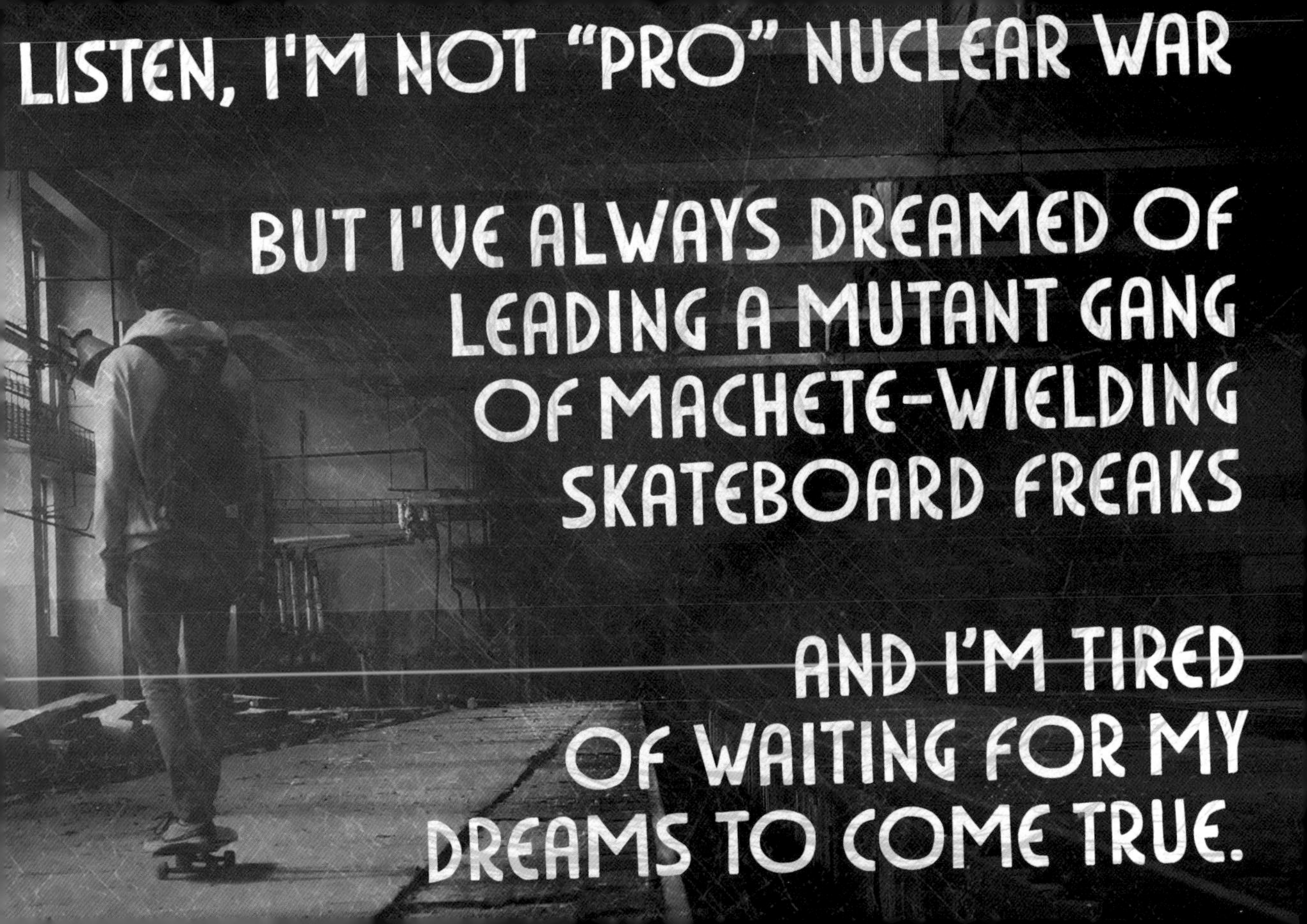
LISTEN, I'M NOT "PRO" NUCLEAR WAR
BUT I'VE ALWAYS DREAMED OF LEADING A MUTANT GANG OF MACHETE-WIELDING SKATEBOARD FREAKS
AND I'M TIRED OF WAITING FOR MY DREAMS TO COME TRUE.

// THIS MYSTERIOUS ISLAND //

NO SHIPS ON THE HORIZON.

NO RESCUE COMING.

JUST YOU AND ME AND THIS MYSTERIOUS ISLAND OF PREHISTORIC MONSTERS HUNGRY FOR BLOOD.

YOU ALWAYS KNOW JUST WHAT TO GET ME FOR MY BIRTHDAY.

// MARY, MARY //

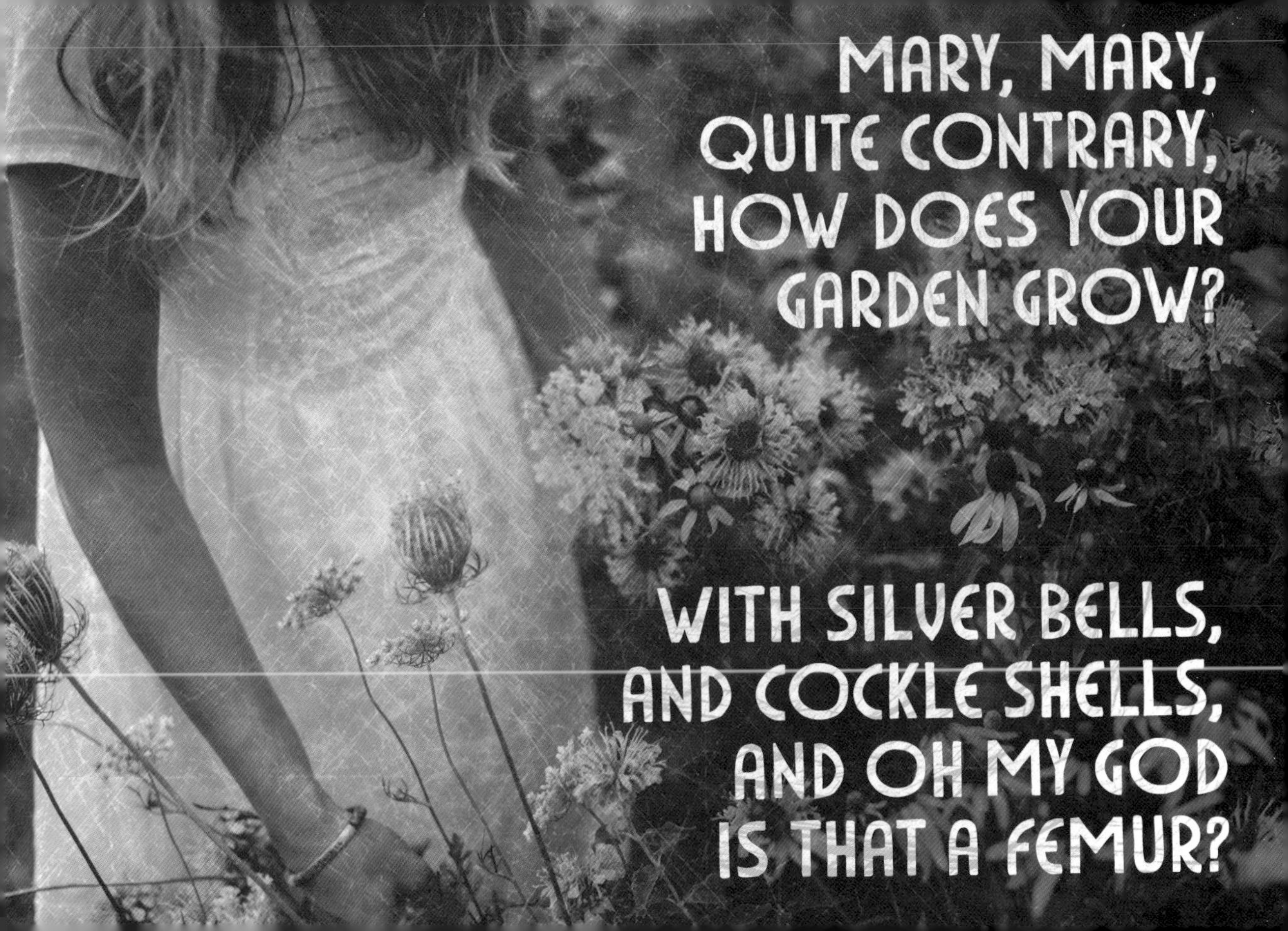

MARY, MARY,
QUITE CONTRARY,
HOW DOES YOUR
GARDEN GROW?

WITH SILVER BELLS,
AND COCKLE SHELLS,
AND OH MY GOD
IS THAT A FEMUR?

// THE BLACKOUT GAME //

ON SUMMER NIGHTS, WHEN THE CITY'S POWER FAILED AND EVERY WINDOW A.C. UNIT GROANED TO A STOP, WE'D RACE UP THE ATTIC STAIRS TO PLAY THE BLACKOUT GAME. CLOSED UP IN THE HEAT, BREATHING IN DUST FROM ANCIENT MOUNDS OF INSULATION SCATTERED ABOUT WARPED FLOORBOARDS, WE SAT AND LISTENED.

FIRST YOU'D HEAR THE ALMOST-SILENCE. MUFFLED VOICES ON THE LANDING BELOW. DISTANT CAR HORNS. A NERVOUS COUGH WITHIN OUR CIRCLE.

THEN, THE SECOND SILENCE — THE ONE BEHIND THE SOFT SOUNDS. IT WAS DARKER, MORE INTIMATE. IT FILLED THE MUSTY ROOM AND PRESSED ITSELF IN CLOSE AROUND US LIKE A FEVER.

ONLY IF YOU STAYED UNTIL THE END WOULD YOU HEAR THE THIRD SILENCE — THE ONE WE NEVER TALKED ABOUT AFTER THE GAME. A NON-SOUND SO DEEP IT CAME FROM INSIDE YOU — LIKE THE SPACE BETWEEN HEARTBEATS, LIKE DREAD ITSELF, LIKE THE HUM OF BLOOD IN YOUR TEMPLES.

ONE BY ONE, AS WE HIT OUR LIMITS, WE'D FLEE THE ATTIC AND GO DOWN TO PLAY TRUTH OR DARE, OR PESTER OUR BELEAGUERED PARENTS AS THEY FANNED THEMSELVES WITH YESTERDAY'S NEWSPAPER.

THE GAME HAD NO WINNER, NO PRIZES. BUT I'M CERTAIN EVERY CHILD WHO CLIMBED UP THOSE ATTIC STAIRS CAME DOWN CARRYING SOMETHING NEW INSIDE THEM.

SOMETHING ANCIENT AND DARK AND RELENTLESSLY SILENT.

SOMETHING WAITING FOR ANOTHER BLACKOUT TO BRING IT OUT AGAIN.

// GREETING
THE FUTURE //

PEOPLE KEEP LOCKING THEIR DOORS AND LISTENING TO THE NEWS TALK ABOUT SEA LEVELS AND COASTAL FLOODING AND CASCADING FAILURES.

I KEEP PUTTING ON MY SNORKEL AND GOING OUT TO GREET THE FUTURE.

// YOUR BODY IN
THE CHURCHYARD //

hear this story narrated by Cecil Baldwin at
shorteststory.com/body

FOR THIRTY YEARS, I BROUGHT YOUR BODY TO THE CHURCHYARD ON NEW-MOON NIGHTS TO ATTEMPT THE RITUAL.

FOR THIRTY YEARS, YOU DID NOT STIR.

IT WASN'T UNTIL THE MEN WITH PICKS AND SHOVELS CAME TO DIG UP THE GROANING EARTH THAT I REALIZED THE RITUAL HAD WORKED EVERY SINGLE TIME.

JUST NOT ON YOU.

// CRY TO SLEEP //

guest story by Shawn Coss

FOR THE PAST FOUR WEEKS, I'VE CRAWLED INTO BED AT NIGHT ONLY TO BE WOKEN UP MOMENTS LATER BY THE CRYING AND WHIMPERING OF MY DAUGHTER. SHE CALLS FOR ME TO COME ROCK HER TO SLEEP.

I KNOW I MUST BE STRONG, AND WAIT IT OUT. LIKE EVERY NIGHT, I TURN THE SOUND MACHINE UP AND TRY TO BLOCK OUT HER VOICE.

I KNOW AFTER A FEW MINUTES IT'LL PASS AND ALL WILL BE SILENT AGAIN, AND I CAN SLEEP. I CALL OUT TO HER THAT IT'S ALRIGHT, AND I'LL SEE HER IN THE MORNING. SHE QUIETS DOWN, AND I CAN SLEEP.

IN THE MORNING, I'LL HAVE MY COFFEE AND HEAD OUTSIDE AND ACROSS THE STREET, WHERE I WALK THROUGH THE CEMETERY TO VISIT MY DAUGHTER'S GRAVE. BECAUSE I KEEP MY PROMISES AND VISIT HER EVERY MORNING.

// THE GRIND //

SOME DAYS, TRYING TO WRITE FEELS LIKE FORCING YOUR OWN ARM THROUGH A MEAT GRINDER.

SOME DAYS IT COMES A LITTLE EASIER,

LIKE FORCING SOMEONE ELSE'S ARM THROUGH A MEAT GRINDER.

// PRESIDENT PENGUIN //

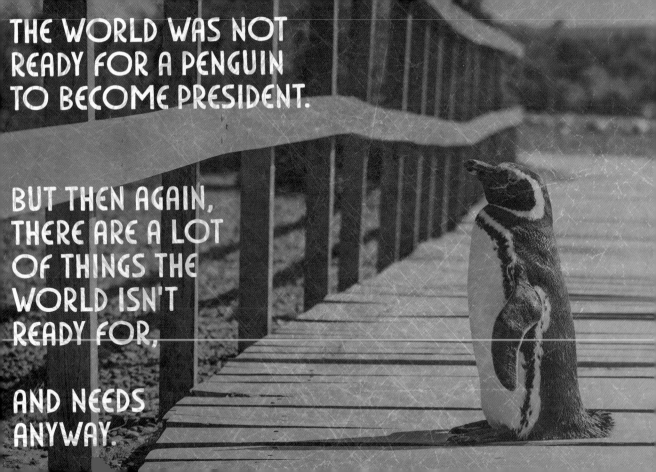

THE WORLD WAS NOT READY FOR A PENGUIN TO BECOME PRESIDENT.

BUT THEN AGAIN, THERE ARE A LOT OF THINGS THE WORLD ISN'T READY FOR,

AND NEEDS ANYWAY.

// RELATIONSHIP STATUS //

hear this story narrated by Cecil Baldwin at
shorteststory.com/relationship

RELATIONSHIP STATUS:

SOUL-BONDED TO A
1,200-YEAR-OLD VIKING
WARLORD'S SCREAMING
GHOST,

HEART PROMISED IN
BLOOD SACRIFICE
TO ANCIENT
MESOPOTAMIAN
FERTILITY DEITY,

LOOKING TO FLIRT.

// RESCUE DOG //

THEY THINK I AM CALLED "RESCUE DOG" BECAUSE
THEY BROUGHT ME HOME, SAVED ME FROM
A DARK PLACE OF RUST AND CONCRETE,
A ROOM THAT HELD NO SMELLS BUT
URINE AND ANGER AND FEAR.

THEY DO NOT KNOW THAT WHEN I DREAM,
I AM ONE HUNDRED FEET TALL.

I AM BRAVE AND SWIFT AND FIERCE,
AND I CHASE AWAY THEIR SADNESS.
I FREE ALL THE SMALL, SCARED THINGS
THEY CAGE UP IN THE DARK PLACES
INSIDE THEM. I WALK THEM OUT OF
THEIR ANGER AND FEAR AND
I BRING THEM HOME.

AND THAT IS WHY I AM
CALLED "RESCUE DOG."

// AWAKE ON THE SUBWAY //

YOU JOLT AWAKE ON THE SUBWAY, TRYING TO REMEMBER WHAT YOU'D BEEN DREAMING ABOUT. YOU WERE RIDING THE TRAIN THROUGH THE DARK WHEN... IT'S ALL SO FUZZY NOW. YOUR HEAD THROBS, AND THE RHYTHMIC LURCH OF THE SUBWAY CAR PUTS A SICK AND SLEEPY FEELING IN YOUR STOMACH. YOUR HEAD STARTS TO NOD. YOU ALMOST DON'T HEAR THE SCREECH AND GRIND AS THE CAR SLIPS LOOSE FROM THE RAILS. JUST BEFORE THE TRAIN CRASHES INTO THE TUNNEL WALL, YOU REMEMBER THAT YOUR DREAM STARTED LIKE THIS:

YOU JOLT AWAKE ON THE SUBWAY, TRYING TO REMEMBER WHAT YOU'D BEEN DREAMING ABOUT. YOU WERE RIDING THE TRAIN THROUGH THE DARK WHEN... IT'S ALL SO FUZZY NOW. YOUR HEAD THROBS, AND THE RHYTHMIC LURCH OF THE SUBWAY CAR PUTS A SICK AND SLEEPY FEELING IN YOUR STOMACH. YOUR HEAD STARTS TO NOD. YOU ALMOST DON'T HEAR THE SCREECH AND GRIND AS THE CAR SLIPS LOOSE FROM THE RAILS. JUST BEFORE THE TRAIN CRASHES INTO THE TUNNEL WALL, YOU REMEMBER THAT YOUR DREAM STARTED LIKE THIS:

YOU JOLT AWAKE ON THE SUBWAY, TRYING TO REMEMBER WHAT YOU'D BEEN DREAMING ABOUT. YOU WERE RIDING THE TRAIN THROUGH THE DARK WHEN... IT'S ALL SO FUZZY NOW. YOUR HEAD THROBS, AND THE RHYTHMIC LURCH OF THE SUBWAY CAR PUTS A SICK AND SLEEPY FEELING IN YOUR STOMACH. YOUR HEAD STARTS TO NOD. YOU ALMOST DON'T HEAR THE SCREECH AND GRIND AS THE CAR SLIPS LOOSE FROM THE RAILS. JUST BEFORE THE TRAIN CRASHES INTO THE TUNNEL WALL, YOU REMEMBER THAT YOUR DREAM STARTED LIKE THIS:

YOU JOLT AWAKE ON THE SUBWAY, TRYING TO REMEMBER WHAT YOU'D BEEN DREAMING ABOUT. YOU WERE RIDING THE TRAIN THROUGH THE DARK WHEN... IT'S ALL SO FUZZY NOW. YOUR HEAD THROBS, AND THE RHYTHMIC LURCH OF THE SUBWAY CAR PUTS A SICK AND SLEEPY FEELING IN YOUR STOMACH. YOUR HEAD STARTS TO NOD. YOU ALMOST DON'T HEAR THE SCREECH AND GRIND AS THE CAR SLIPS LOOSE FROM THE RAILS. JUST BEFORE THE TRAIN CRASHES INTO THE TUNNEL WALL, YOU REMEMBER THAT YOUR DREAM STARTED LIKE THIS:

YOU JOLT AWAKE ON THE SUBWAY, TRYING TO REMEMBER WHAT YOU'D BEEN DREAMING ABOUT. YOU WERE RIDING THE TRAIN THROUGH THE DARK WHEN... IT'S ALL SO FUZZY NOW. YOUR HEAD THROBS, AND THE RHYTHMIC LURCH OF THE SUBWAY CAR PUTS A SICK AND SLEEPY FEELING IN YOUR STOMACH. YOUR HEAD STARTS TO NOD. YOU ALMOST DON'T HEAR THE SCREECH AND GRIND AS THE CAR SLIPS LOOSE FROM THE RAILS. JUST BEFORE THE TRAIN CRASHES INTO THE TUNNEL WALL, YOU REMEMBER THAT YOUR DREAM STARTED LIKE THIS:

YOU JOLT AWAKE ON THE SUBWAY, TRYING TO REMEMBER WHAT YOU'D BEEN DREAMING ABOUT. YOU WERE RIDING THE TRAIN THROUGH THE DARK WHEN... IT'S ALL SO FUZZY NOW. YOUR HEAD THROBS, AND THE RHYTHMIC LURCH OF THE SUBWAY CAR PUTS A SICK AND SLEEPY FEELING IN YOUR STOMACH. YOUR HEAD STARTS TO NOD. YOU ALMOST DON'T HEAR THE SCREECH AND GRIND AS THE CAR SLIPS LOOSE FROM THE RAILS. JUST BEFORE THE TRAIN CRASHES INTO THE TUNNEL WALL, YOU REMEMBER HOW YOUR DREAM STARTED.

// A SMALLER WORLD //

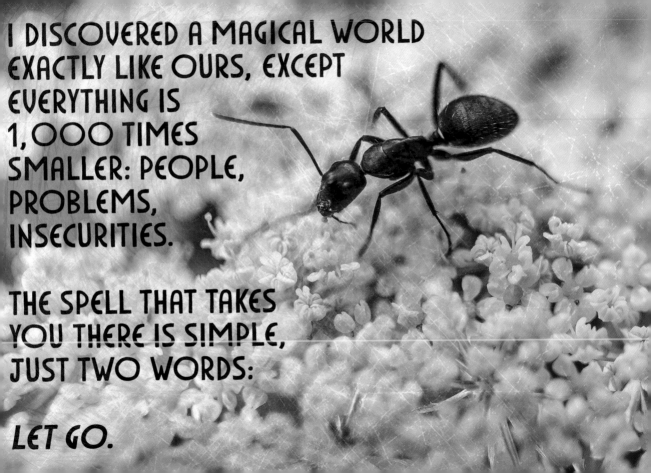

I DISCOVERED A MAGICAL WORLD
EXACTLY LIKE OURS, EXCEPT
EVERYTHING IS
1,000 TIMES
SMALLER: PEOPLE,
PROBLEMS,
INSECURITIES.

THE SPELL THAT TAKES
YOU THERE IS SIMPLE,
JUST TWO WORDS:

LET GO.

// AN ENEMY
WE CAN KILL //

THE DEAD RULE THIS LAND NOW.
THEY CHASE US DOWN EMPTY STREETS
AND ABANDONED HIGHWAYS SPLIT
WITH CRACKS AND OVERGROWTH.

AT FIRST IT WAS STRANGE TO
BE MAKING OUR WAY IN A
WORLD WITHOUT THE HUM
OF WIRES AND CARS
AND DEADLINES.

BUT IT'S A RELIEF TO
FINALLY BE LOOKING
OVER OUR SHOULDERS
FOR AN ENEMY
WE CAN KILL.

// TALKING WITH FISH //

THE ACCIDENT GAVE ME
THE POWER TO
TALK TO FISH

WITHOUT
THE SOCIAL SKILLS
TO MAKE THEM LIKE ME.

// AFTER THE MAN-WOLF BIT ME //

hear this story narrated by Cecil Baldwin at
shorteststory.com/wolf

AFTER THE MAN-WOLF BIT ME, I EXPERIENCED A
TERRIBLE TRANSFORMATION.

NOW, WHEN THE FULL MOON RISES, MY FLESH
SHUDDERS AND MY BONES CRACK AND MY BODY
REBUILDS ITSELF INTO THIS GROTESQUE NEW SHAPE:

A MOUTH FULL OF TEETH THAT CANNOT BITE,

A STOMACH THAT GETS SICK AT THE TASTE OF BLOOD,

A SPINE MADE FOR HUNCHING OVER AN OFFICE DESK.

// DOING WITCHCRAFT //

guest story by Sandra Kasturi

THERE'S A SECRET TO DOING WITCHCRAFT:
IT'S IN THE COUNTING, IT'S IN THE RHYMING.

"ONE, TWO, BUCKLE MY SHOE" IS A SPELL,
NOT SOMETHING FOR THE NURSERY.

MOTHER GOOSE IS A GRIMOIRE, AND ALL SMALL
CHILDREN PRACTISE MAGIC, THEIR CONFLICTING
TANTRUMS AND NEEDS BATTLING ACROSS THE
LANDS AND CENTURIES OF OUR SPECIES.

WHY DO YOU THINK THE WORLD IS
THE WAY IT IS?

// MIRACLE PLANET //

I MISS HOW THE AIR TASTED BEFORE THE
REBREATHERS,

HOW THE SKY LOOKED BEFORE THE PANELS OF
THE TERRA-DOME BROKE IT INTO A THOUSAND
GLEAMING HEXAGONS,

HOW A SUNRISE COULD WARM MY SKIN WITH A
BEAM OF UNBROKEN LIGHT FROM A STAR
150 MILLION KILOMETRES AWAY,

HOW IT FELT TO WAKE UP ON THIS MIRACLE
PLANET BEFORE WE TURNED IT AGAINST US.

// THE LITERALLY SPELL //

THE WIZARD'S SPELL MADE IT SO ANYONE WHO SAID
"LITERALLY" HAD THEIR WORDS COME TRUE.

HE WANTED TO TEACH US NOT TO
EXAGGERATE OR MISUSE LANGUAGE.

INSTEAD WE REBUILT THE WORLD
WITH IMPOSSIBLE
SUPERLATIVES AND
RECKLESS METAPHORS.

WE MADE HIM EAT HIS WORDS.

LITERALLY.

// THE GHOST ON THE BAY //

ON A CALM, CLEAR NIGHT, I SEE HIS GHOST OUT ON THE BAY.

ON A CALM, CLEAR NIGHT, I LOOK OUT AND WONDER IF HE SEEMS CLOSER NOW THAN HE DID THE NIGHT BEFORE.

ON A CALM, CLEAR NIGHT, HE REACHES THE SHORE BELOW MY COTTAGE AND HIS FACE IS CLOSE ENOUGH FOR ME TO LOOK INTO EYES THAT SWALLOW MOONLIGHT.

ON A CALM, CLEAR NIGHT, I SIT IN THE CHAIR BY THE DOOR WAITING FOR HIS KNOCK, KNOWING I WILL HAVE NO CHOICE BUT TO RISE AND LET HIM IN, AND IT IS THE CALMEST, CLEAREST THOUGHT I HAVE EVER KNOWN.

// THE BOTTOM OF THE NIGHTMARE //

HER NIGHTMARES GOT WORSE, SO I BUILT A DIVING SUIT TO EXPLORE THE RESTLESS OCEAN OF HER DREAMS.

I THOUGHT IT WOULD BE BLACK AND FULL OF MONSTERS, LIKE STEPPING THROUGH THE GASOLINE RAINBOW ON TOP OF A PUDDLE AND ENTERING A WORLD OF DARK REFLECTIONS AND BROKEN COLOURS.

I WAS WRONG.

HER DREAM WAS WHITE AND ENDLESS, A WORLD SO VAST AND BRIGHT AND EMPTY THAT NOTHING COULD HIDE.

IT WAS THERE, AT THE BOTTOM OF THE NIGHTMARE, I LEARNED THAT TERROR IS NOT MEETING A MONSTER IN THE DARK.

IT IS MEETING OURSELVES IN THE LIGHT.

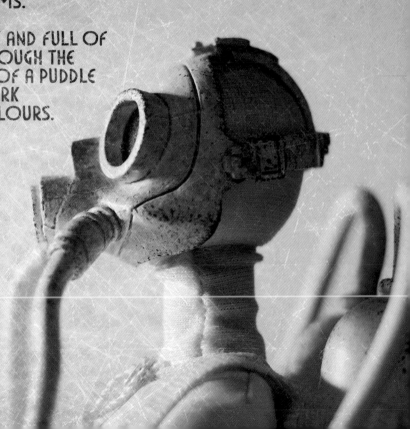

I LOVE WATCHING THE NEWS TRY TO EXPLAIN THE SUDDEN APPEARANCE OF THE MYSTERY OBELISK.

THEY BRING IN EXPERTS AND COMMENTATORS AND HISTORIANS AND SYMBOLOGISTS AND OBELISK SPECIALISTS AND IT ALL BECOMES SO CLEAR:

THEY HAVE NO IDEA WHAT THEY'RE TALKING ABOUT.

NONE OF US EVER HAVE.

// THE WAY
WITH STORIES //

IN THE OLD DAYS, MONSTERS HAD NO WEAKNESSES.

VAMPIRES DID NOT FEAR STAKES NOR CROSSES. WEREWOLVES DID NOT RECOIL AT THE TOUCH OF SILVER. WE HAD NO WEAPONS WITH WHICH TO STRIKE BACK AT THE DARKNESS.

EXCEPT FOR OUR STORIES.

OUR STORIES MADE THEM MORTAL. SOMEONE SPUN A YARN THAT A STAKE COULD STOP THE HEART OF VAMPIRE, AND SOMEONE ELSE TOLD SOMEONE ELSE, UNTIL IT WAS TRUE. MAYBE IT HAD ALWAYS BEEN TRUE. MAYBE IT BECAME TRUE IN THE TELLING.

WE TOLD STORIES UNTIL THESE MONSTERS WERE MORE FAMOUS FOR THEIR WEAKNESSES THAN FOR THEIR STRENGTHS, UNTIL WE NO LONGER BELIEVED THEY HAD EVER BEEN REAL IN THE FIRST PLACE. AND IN ITS OWN WAY, THAT WAS TRUE TOO.

FOR THAT IS THE WAY WITH STORIES.

WE CANNOT BE SURE WHEN THEY STOP TELLING THE TRUTH, AND WHEN THEY BEGIN TO CREATE IT.

// THE REEF OF WISHES //

WE FOUND A MAGICAL REEF WHERE
THE FISH GRANT WISHES.

WE WISHED FIRST FOR MORE WISHES,
THEN FOR FASTER CARS
AND TALLER CITIES
AND SOFTER LIVES.

BY THE TIME WE THOUGHT TO USE OUR WISHES ON
CLIMATE CHANGE AND OCEAN ACIDIFICATION,

THERE WERE NO FISH LEFT TO GRANT THEM.

// INDIANA //

guest story by Sonya Ballantyne,
dedicated to Gladys George-Ballantyne

MY MUM ONCE TOLD ME ABOUT A LEGENDARY HERO NAMED INDIANA JONES.

FOR A WEIRD GIRL AND HER STANDOFFISH MUM, INDY'S ADVENTURES BROUGHT US CLOSER TOGETHER.

I DID NOT NOTICE UNTIL LATER BUT THESE ADVENTURES SEEMED LIKE MY MUM'S MESSAGE TO ME ON HOW TO SURVIVE AN UNJUST WORLD IN A WAY SHE COULD NOT VERBALIZE. THE MOST IMPORTANT LESSON I EVER LEARNED AS AN INDIAN GIRL WAS:

"YOU LOST TODAY, KID, BUT THAT DOESN'T MEAN YOU HAVE TO LIKE IT."

// ANGELS IN DISGUISE //

*hear this story narrated by Cecil Baldwin at
shorteststory.com/angel*

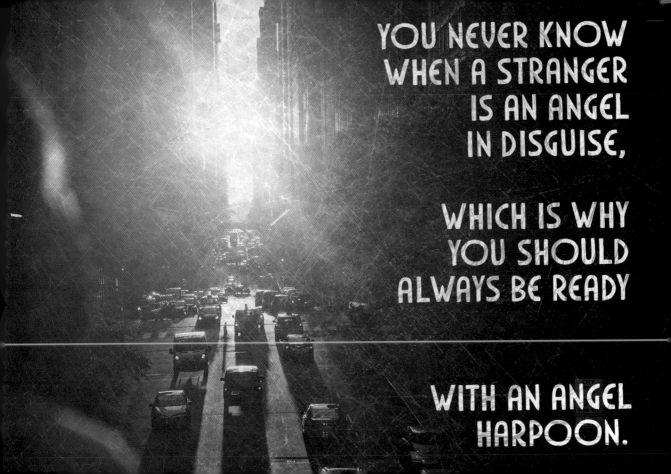

YOU NEVER KNOW
WHEN A STRANGER
IS AN ANGEL
IN DISGUISE,

WHICH IS WHY
YOU SHOULD
ALWAYS BE READY

WITH AN ANGEL
HARPOON.

// WET, RED KNIVES //

WHEN THE SUPERMARKET SHELVES
WERE PICKED BARE, WE STARTED
HUNTING IN THE RUINS.

WHEN THE DEER AND RABBITS DIED OUT,
WE ATE RACCOONS. THEN PIGEONS.
THEN RATS.

WHEN THE RATS WENT,
WE LOOKED AT EACH OTHER,
AT OUR WET, RED KNIVES,
AND KNEW:

FOOD IS ANYTHING
YOU ARE HUNGRY ENOUGH
TO EAT.

// ENDGAME //

WHILE I SLEEP, SOMEBODY IS SHIFTING CITY BLOCKS LIKE THE FACES OF A RUBIK'S CUBE. EVERY MORNING I FIND STREETS AND BUILDINGS HAVE RELOCATED. YESTERDAY MY APARTMENT OVERLOOKED A SUNNY PARK. TODAY, I FACE A DEPARTMENT STORE AS I EAT BREAKFAST. I ASK MY NEIGHBOUR, WHO TELLS ME IT'S ALWAYS BEEN THIS WAY.

I TRY TO TRACK THE CHANGES ON A TRANSIT MAP, BUT BY THE NEXT DAY, THOSE COLOURED LINES HAVE CHANGED TOO, AND NO ONE SEEMS TO NOTICE OR CARE.

THE ONLY TRUE MAP IS MY MIND, AND OH HOW THE PIECES WHIRL. AFTER A WEEK, I CAN ALMOST SEE THE SHAPE OF IT: HOW THE BUILDINGS ADVANCE AND RETREAT WITH THE EBB AND FLOW OF CONCRETE. IT'S NOT A RUBIK'S CUBE — IT'S A CHESSBOARD. I AM DETERMINED TO UNCOVER WHATEVER INVISIBLE HAND IS PLAYING WITH US, AND WHATEVER STRANGE ENDGAME IT MOVES US TOWARD.

I LOCK MYSELF ON THE ROOF WITH CIGARETTES AND CHEWING GUM, AND STARE UP AT THE SKY, WAITING. AFTER THREE DAYS, THE SUN STOPS SETTING. MY EYES ACHE. I TRACK TIME BY MY WATCH. AFTER FIVE DAYS, THE CLOUDS VANISH AND THE BLUE TURNS THE FLAT GREY OF A SCREEN SAVING POWER. AFTER A WEEK, A VOICE CALLS OUT FROM ABOVE.

THIS CAN'T GO ON.

AND I BEGIN TO FLOAT UPWARD, UP OVER THE SKYSCRAPERS AND PARKS AND ALL THE OBLIVIOUS PEOPLE, UNTIL THE GREY TAKES ME IN AND THE ONLY THOUGHT LEFT IN MY BRAIN IS KNOWING THAT I WAS RIGHT, SURELY I WAS RIGHT.

FULLER L

// SUCK IT, HEMINGWAY //

FOR SALE:

BABY SHOES.

HAUNTED!

// LITTLE WHITE HOUSE //

IN THE SNOW-COVERED VALLEY SITS A LITTLE WHITE HOUSE, WHERE MANY GO IN BUT NO ONE COMES OUT.

PEOPLE GO THERE WHEN THE SICKNESS CLAIMS THEM. MY SISTER LEFT LAST WEEK. I BEGGED HER TO STAY BUT HER EYES LOOKED PAST ME AND THE STORM DID NOT TOUCH HER AS SHE WALKED OUT OF THE VILLAGE AND THE SNOW SWALLOWED HER FOOTSTEPS.

YESTERDAY, I BREWED HOT TEA AND STRUGGLED THROUGH THE SQUALL UNTIL I ENTERED A STRANGE VALLEY WHERE NO WIND STIRS AND NO BIRDS SING AND SILENCE COVERS THE WORLD LIKE FRESH SNOW. I STOOD OUTSIDE THE LITTLE WHITE HOUSE AND LOOKED THROUGH THE DARKENED WINDOW. FOR A MOMENT I SAW A FACE, STRANGE AND PALLID. A FACE SO FAMILIAR. NOT LIKE MY SISTER'S FACE, BUT LIKE MY OWN.

I RAN ALL THE WAY HOME.

THIS MORNING I WOKE WITH FEVER AND CHILLS. I DREAM NOW, EVEN WHEN I AM AWAKE. I SEE THE HOUSE. THE FACE IN THE WINDOW. THE DOOR OPENS AND TWO THIN, PALE ARMS INVITE ME IN.

NOW I KNOW MY HOME HAS NEVER BEEN HERE IN THE VILLAGE, AMONG THESE PEOPLE WHO LIVE IN FEAR OF STORMS AND SICKNESS AND DARKENED WINDOWS.

MY HOME HAS ALWAYS BEEN OUT IN THE VALLEY, IN THE SILENCE OF A LITTLE WHITE HOUSE, WHERE MANY GO IN BUT NO ONE COMES OUT.

// UNMADE FOR US //

hear this story narrated by Cecil Baldwin at
shorteststory.com/unmade

THE WORLD WE REMEMBER IS GONE, EVERYONE WE KNOW IS DEAD, BUT I AM IN LOVE WITH THESE STRANGE DAWNS, HOW THE SUN STRUGGLES TO FIND US THROUGH THE HAZE EVERY MORNING,

AND LIGHTS UP A WORLD UNMADE JUST FOR US.

// **THE SHORTEST STORY** //

hear this story narrated by Cecil Baldwin at
shorteststory.com/story

AN OLD MAN APPROACHES YOU WITH A BOOK IN HIS HAND.

SOMETHING IN HIS CRINKLED EYES TELLS YOU IT IS A BOOK HE HAS READ MANY TIMES BEFORE, ALTHOUGH ITS SPINE IS CRISP AND UNCRACKED, AS IF IT HAS COME ALL THIS WAY AND WAITED ALL THIS TIME FOR YOU TO REACH OUT AND OPEN IT.

HE HANDS YOU THE BOOK. THE TOME IS SOFT AND STRANGE AND BEAUTIFUL, AND EVERY PAGE YOU TURN REVEALS A DIFFERENT STORY, A TALE SO INCREDIBLE AND TRUE THAT IT REMINDS OF YOU OF SOMETHING THAT NEVER HAPPENED TO YOU, BUT STILL YOU CANNOT FORGET.

EACH PAGE IS A POSTCARD YOU HAVE SENT TO YOURSELF FROM ANOTHER LIFE, FROM AN IMPOSSIBLE WORLD, FROM A PLACE YOU HAVE NEVER BEEN BUT ALWAYS REMEMBERED.

AND WHEN YOU REACH THE END AND THERE IS A STORY IN WHICH YOU MEET AN OLD MAN WHO GIVES YOU A STRANGE AND BEAUTIFUL BOOK. YOU LOOK UP FROM READING AND THE OLD MAN IS GONE. THERE IS ONLY YOU AND THE BOOK, YOU AND THESE PAGES OF STRANGE AND BEAUTIFUL LIVES YOU NEVER LIVED.

THIS IS THE SHORTEST STORY, AND IT IS YOURS TO KEEP

// THAT'S ALL, FOLKS //

// ACKNOWLEDGEMENTS //

There are a great many people to thank for the existence of this book, first and foremost being my friend and editor Sandra Kasturi, who always pushed me to write more strangely, more boldly, and more often, as well as my friend and mentor Darryl Whetter, who taught me to write like every word matters, because every word does.

I never would have started *The Shortest Story* without Joey Comeau and Emily Horne's trailblazing work on *A Softer World*, and I wouldn't have carried on with the same reckless fervour if it weren't for the friends, family, and readers who took time to let me know this weird little project was speaking to them. (Even if the things it was saying were disturbing.)

I can't tell you which demon I had to cheat in a game of Egyptian ratscrew to gain the supernaturally good luck that has surrounded me with such kind, creative, long-suffering humans, but I can say this: there is no greater magic than the company of people who want to see you succeed.

I also owe special thanks to my collaborators: Cecil Baldwin (the voice in my head as I wrote so many of these stories); the guest authors (many of whom inspired me to begin this project); the proofreaders (Brett Savory, Kate Lane-Smith, Megan Harris, and Eric Weiss); and the many incredible photographers who have made their work freely available for strange projects such as this. Your generosity and talent humbles me.

// ABOUT THE AUTHOR //

Peter Chiykowski is a full-time writer, illustrator, and musician, and a part-time rabble-rouser.

His webcomic *Rock, Paper, Cynic* won the Aurora Award for "Best Graphic Novel" and his comics, poems and writing projects have appeared in *Entertainment Weekly, Newsweek, Huffington Post, Asimov's Science Fiction, Best Canadian Poetry,* and *Imaginarium: Best Canadian Speculative Writing.* He also writes stories for *EMBERWIND,* a new tabletop RPG.

When Peter is not writing strange stories, he's being dragged by rescue and foster dogs on long walks in Toronto parks.

// GUEST AUTHORS //

A very special thanks goes to the guest authors in this volume:

Sonya Ballantyne
code-breaker-films.com

Shawn Coss
shawncossart.com

Sandra Kasturi
sandrakasturi.com

Helen Marshall
helen-marshall.com

James Mark Miller
asmallfiction.com

Robert Shearman
robertshearman.com

Jordan Shiveley
voidmerch.net

// PHOTOGRAPHERS //

Special thanks goes to Inna Yasinska, whose breathtaking photography was a major inspiration for starting this project, and whose work appears our times in this volume.

I must also thank all the artists and photographers who make their work available for creative inspiration and commercial use through sites like Unsplash. There's no way I could make *The Shortest Story* without you.

From front to back, this book uses the work of the following talented photographers:

Leo Fosdal (cover), Medhat Ayad (dedication), Tim Marshall (foreword), Adria Berrocal Forcada, Christian Bardenhorst, Aziz Acharki, Jeremy Bishop, Patrick Hendry, Aimee Vogelsang, Brooklyn Morgan, Jeremy Bishop, Jonny Caspari, Autumn Mooney,

Pixabay, MontyLov, Felix Russell-Saw, NASA, Jürgen Jester, Mohammad Metri, Tim Foster, Samuel Zeller, Inna Yasinska, Abhay Singh, SpaceX, Kinga Chichewicz, Kristina Paukshtite, Vidar Nordli Mathisen, Marc-Olivier Jodoin, Anthony Delanoix, Allef Vinicius, Delfi de la Rua, pxhere, Vianka Merano, Antoine Beauvillain, Peter Chiykowski, Eugene Zhang, Blair Fraser, Aziz Acharki, Matthew Larkin, Craig Strahorn, Ashim d'Silva, Matthew Henry, Inna Yasinska, Davide Ragusa, Sai Kiran Anagani, Tina Hartung, Tuur Tisseghem, Jaredd Craig, Marat Gilyadzinov, Christopher Windus, Clem Onojeghuo, Eric Ward, Jeremy Bishop, Anthony Delanoix, Mike Wilson, Ferdinand Stöhr, Christal Yuen, Markus Spiske, Jacky Chiu, Stefan Stefancik, Adam Krowitz, Samantha Gades, Erik Witsoe, Jakob Owens, Yuriy Garnaev, Joanna Malinowska, Florian Klauer, Giorgio Parravicini, Rob Potter, Patrick Hendry, Sachit Rathi, David Higgins, Alexandre Perotto, Talia Cohen, Ben Rosett, Markus Clemens, drmakete lab, Alejandro Alvarez, Lukas Robertson, Siyan Ren, Jon Tyson, Lukas Neasi, Alexandra Rose, Sven Scheuermeier, The Vantage Point, Victor Larracuente, Inna Yasinska, Janko Ferlic, maxpixel, Aaron VanPoole, Jez Timms, Inna Yasinska (author photo).

*new short stories
every week at*

SHORTESTSTORY.COM